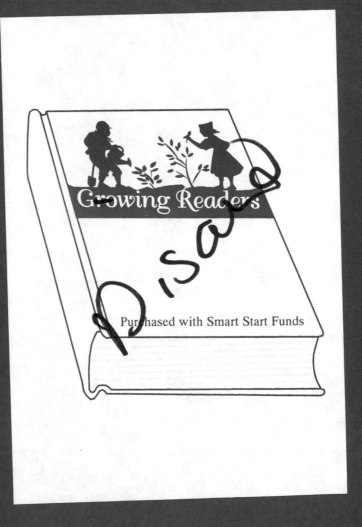

Pets!

Melrose Cooper

pictures by

Yumi Heo

Henry Holt and Company · New York

Pets from around the Globe

For Hannah Kroll-Haeick and her pets, big and small, one and all
— M. C.

In loving memory of Minnie
— Y. H.

Henry Holt and Company, Inc., *Publishers since 1866*
115 West 18th Street, New York, New York 10011

Henry Holt is a registered trademark of Henry Holt and Company, Inc.
Text copyright © 1998 by Melrose Cooper. Illustrations copyright © 1998 by Yumi Heo
All rights reserved.
Published in Canada by Fitzhenry & Whiteside Ltd., 195 Allstate Parkway, Markham, Ontario L3R 4T8.

Library of Congress Cataloging-in-Publication Data
Cooper, Melrose.
Pets! / by Melrose Cooper; pictures by Yumi Heo.
Summary: A child contemplates the wide variety of pets available at a pet show,
from furry and purry to feathered and tethered.
[1. Pets—Fiction. 2. Pet shows—Fiction. 3. Stories in rhyme.]
I. Heo, Yumi, ill. II. Title.
PZ8.3.C788Pi 1998 [E]—dc21 97-16173
ISBN 0-8050-3893-0 / First Edition—1998
Printed in the United States of America on acid-free paper.∞
The artist used mixed media on watercolor paper to create
the illustrations for this book.
10 9 8 7 6 5 4 3 2 1

What pet
Can I get?
I'm not quite ready yet.

Let me think.
Let me see.
Mmmm. It's all up to me.

A small pet
A tall pet
A curled-in-a-
ball pet.

A furry pet
A purry pet
A skitter-and-scurry pet.

Sleek pets
Slick pets
Do - amazing - tricks pets.

Pawing pets
Cawing pets
Heeing-and-hawing pets

Floppy pets
Hoppy pets
Seed-dropping-sloppy pets.

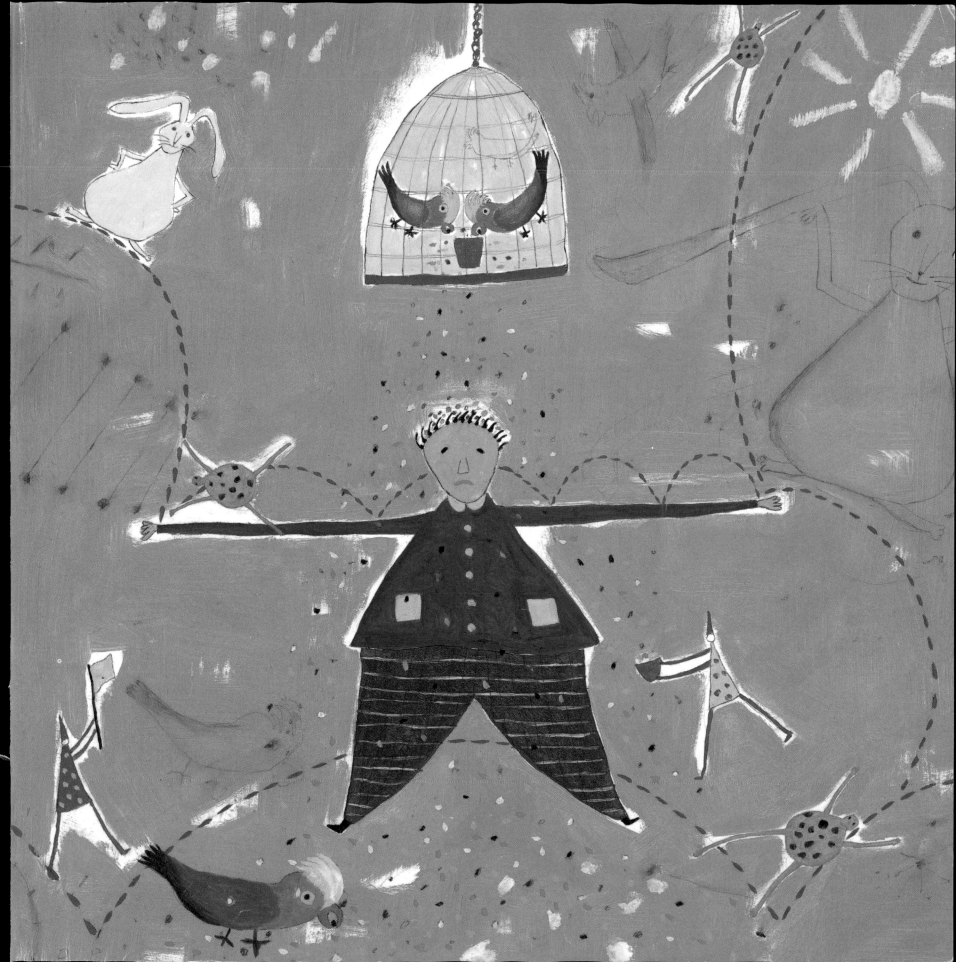

Kissing pets
Hissing pets
Even tail-missing pets.

Tails for Sale

Burrrrp

Burrrp

Burrrp

Chirping pets
Burping pets
Sloshing-and-slurping pets.

Chirp

Chirp

Chirp

Tiny pets
Shiny pets
Prickly-and-spiny pets.

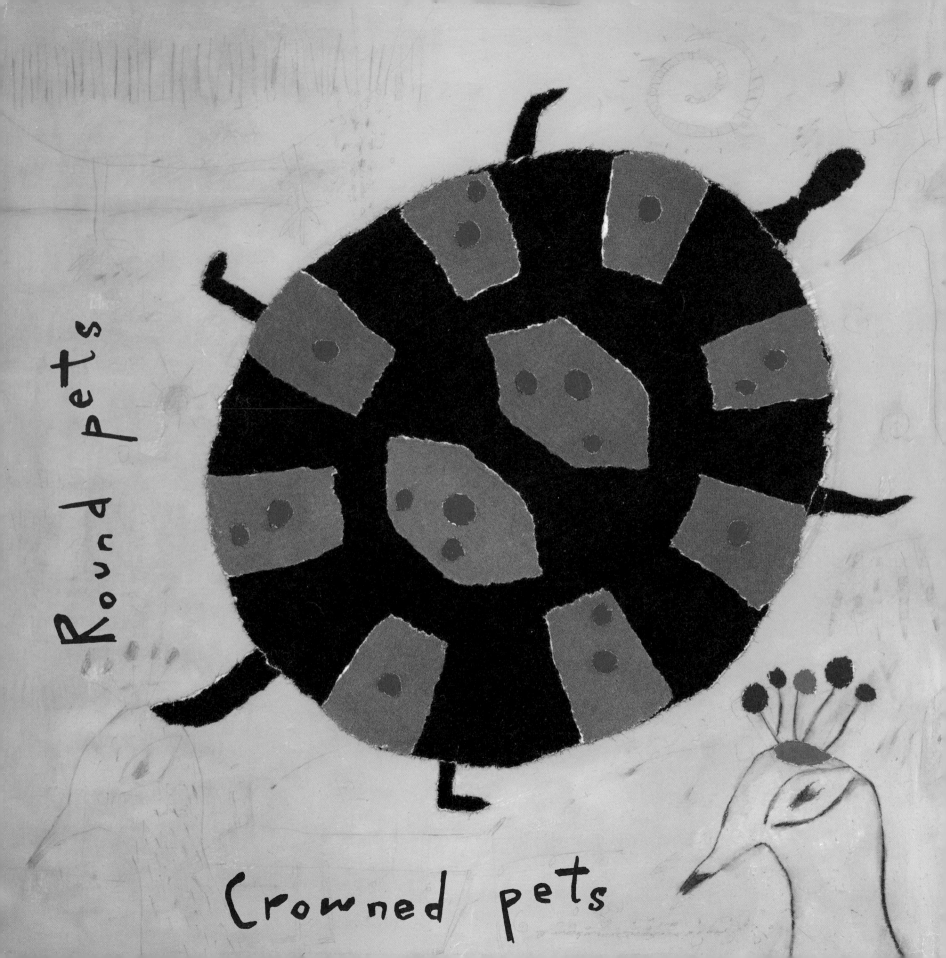

Round pets

Crowned pets

Coiling-around pets.

Neighing pets
Laying pets
Kneeling-and-praying pets.

Tethered pets

All-kinds-of-weather pets.

Feathered pets

Pet Rock

A young pet

An old pet
A have-and-to-hold pet.

A happy-as-can-be pet
A perfect-fit-for-me pet!